W9-CTE-456

A Robbie Reader

MONEY MATTERS: A KID'S GUIDE TO MONEY

A KID'S GUIDE TO EARNING MONEY

Tamra Orr

Mitchell Lane
PUBLISHERS

P.O. Box 196
Hockessin, Delaware 19707

Visit

Comm   .com

MONEY MATTERS
A KID'S GUIDE TO MONEY

Budgeting for Kids

Coins and Other Currency

A Kid's Guide to Earning Money

A Kid's Guide to Stock Market Investing

Savings Tips for Kids

ABOUT THE AUTHOR: Tamra Orr is the author of more than 100 books for children of all ages. She lives in the Pacific Northwest with her kids and husband and spends as much time reading as she possibly can. Being an author is definitely her favorite way to earn money, but she started out with lemonade sales when she was in elementary school. Since then, she has held a number of jobs, from secretary to teacher.

PUBLISHER'S NOTE: The facts on which the story in this book is based have been thoroughly researched. Documentation of such research can be found on page 44. While every possible effort has been made to ensure accuracy, the publisher will not assume liability for damages caused by inaccuracies in the data, and makes no warranty on the accuracy of the information contained herein.

Library of Congress Cataloging-in-Publication Data

Orr, Tamra.
 A kid's guide to earning money / by Tamra Orr.
     p. cm.—(Money matters—a kid's guide to money)
 Includes bibliographical references and index.
 ISBN 978-1-58415-643-7 (library bound)
 1. Money-making projects for children—Juvenile literature. 2. Children—Finance, Personal—Juvenile literature. I. Title.
 HF5392.O77 2009
 650.12083—dc22
                                        2008002253

Printing 1 2 3 4 5 6 7 8 9

PLB

Contents

MOVING UP THE MOUNTAIN

Chapter

1

Mr. Franks' fifth-grade students trickled into the room. The bell would ring any second, and they wanted to be in their seats, or at least close to them, when it did. Mr. Franks was strict when it came to being on time.

"Why do we have a cutout of a mountain on our felt board?" asked Philip, pointing to a large display board next to the teacher's desk.

Carlos shrugged. "I don't know. It looks like there's a hiker at the bottom of it, though."

Philip looked closer. There was a felt hiker at the base of the mountain. It looked like a girl.

"What are you looking at?" asked Leah, coming up behind the boys. Just as Carlos was about to answer, Mr. Franks called the class to attention.

After taking attendance, he smiled at his students. "All right, everyone, meet Astrid," he said, holding up the figure of the hiker. "We are going to help her hike up this tall mountain. If

she reaches the top by the end of the school year, she will be happy—and you will be even happier."

"Why?" asked Melanie.

"Here's the plan," the teacher replied. "We are all going to work together to raise some money, and for every ten dollars we earn, Astrid gets to climb up another step." Mr. Franks showed them what he meant. There were small lines drawn on the edge of the mountain, and each one stood for $10. "When Astrid reaches the top of the mountain, she gets to rest, and we will have earned enough to take a trip to . . ." He paused. Everyone waited.

". . . the new science museum!" he finished.

"You mean the one with the cooking lab?" asked Tomás, "and the hands-on experiment room—and the maze?"

Astrid has a long trip ahead of her, but with everyone's help, she should reach the top just in time for an exciting trip for the whole class.

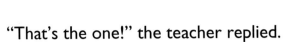

"That's the one!" the teacher replied.

"I thought it wasn't opening until August," said Melanie.

"To the public, you are right," agreed Mr. Franks. "However, they said they would take school groups early . . . plus the head of the museum, Mr. Hamilton, is a good friend of mine. In fact, he used to be my fifth-grade teacher."

Everyone began buzzing about what they each had heard about this new museum. Linda had heard it was the biggest museum in the whole state. Carter's brother had told him that it had robots inside. Mohinder said he had read an article in the newspaper about it. There was supposed to be a real science lab in the museum, complete with glass beakers of bubbling potions.

Kathleen raised her hand. "Mr. Franks, how are we going to earn this money for the museum trip?" she asked.

"I knew someone would ask that," he replied. "First, let's look at how much we need."

He drew a chart on the blackboard.

$_____ x _____ students = cost of getting into the museum

"Okay," said Mr. Franks, turning to face the students again. "Let's figure this out. Mr. Hamilton told me the entrance fee is $3.50 per student." He filled in the first blank.

$3.50 x _____ students = cost of getting into the museum

"Next, we need to figure out how many students are in the class." Everyone swiveled around and started counting. It didn't take long for most of them to lose count and start laughing.

"Let's try that again," suggested Mr. Franks. This time, students counted quietly to themselves.

"Thirty-four," said Rhonda.

"No, thirty-five," disagreed Lucas. "Remember, Jorge is absent today."

"That's right," said Mr. Franks. "He is, so let's add thirty-five to the second blank. Now, what's the product?"

Pencils flew across paper as students raced to see who could come up with the correct answer first.

"I've got it," said Philip. "One hundred twenty-two dollars and fifty cents."

"Exactly," agreed Mr. Franks. "So here is what we have now—"

$3.50 x 35 students =
$122.50

Mr. Franks showed the students exactly how much money they would need to earn to get Astrid to the top of the mountain—and the class to the new science museum.

"We know how much we need to buy our tickets, so what's next?" asked the teacher.

"Are there any other costs we need to know about?" asked Mia.

"Another great question," replied Mr. Franks. "We are using a school bus to get there and back, so our transportation is free. You might want to bring money for the gift shop or to buy a snack, but the amount we have to have is $122.50. For every $10 we earn toward the trip, Astrid  will go one step up the mountain. Now, what is the next step we have to take?"

"We ask our parents for the money," suggested Lyndsay.

"Hmmm. We could do that," said Mr. Franks. "But I would like to see us earn the money instead. Not everyone will be able to earn the same amount, but this is a team effort! We all help each other."

"We need to brainstorm ways we can earn it," suggested Carlos.

"Perfect," said Mr. Franks. He erased the numbers and got ready to make a list. For the next hour, the class came up with many new ideas. By the time the bell rang, the blackboard was full of possibilities. All of them were interesting, but while some of them were reasonable, a few would be impossible.

- Have a yard sale to sell stuff you don't need anymore, such as clothes, toys, or books
- Turn in soda cans or bottles at a recycling center
- Go door-to-door asking for donations
- Sell my sister/brother
- Sell handmade crafts or baked goods
- Hold a telethon on the local TV station
- Turn in our allowances
- Mow lawns for the neighbors
- Get babysitting jobs
- Take a newspaper route
- Do extra chores at home for money
- Rent out our pets
- Hold a car wash

"Mr. Franks, this is a little like getting a job to pay for the things you need, isn't it?" asked Jason.

"That it is! I'm glad you noticed. You will find out, through this experience, that having a job can be wonderful—and sometimes demanding."

According to the U.S. Department of Agriculture, it costs more than $500,000 to raise a child to the age of 17 today. That's a half million dollars!

Just then the bell rang for the next class.

"Keep thinking about new ideas," encouraged Mr. Franks as his students filed out. Soon, the classroom was empty. Mr. Franks looked at the list and chuckled. He knew that with this much determination and imagination, his class would not only go to the museum, but they would have fun earning the money to get there!

TO WORK OR NOT TO WORK

Have you ever worked for money? Maybe you have helped someone in your family or a friend and they paid you for your time and effort. Perhaps you earn an allowance for chores you do around the house. Earning money is often hard work, but it can be nice to have the money you need when you need it!

It is exciting to be able to earn your own money. You might find yourself imagining all the ways you could spend it. If you do, don't worry. Even adults do this!

Finding the Time

It takes a huge commitment to start any kind of job. A person has to be able to fit the job in with his or her other responsibilities, including school, sports, and time with friends and family. Do you think you will have enough time for that? Even if you can't get a steady job for several years, you can give it some serious thought now. It will show you how much free time you have for taking on some extra household chores or helping out friends— to make a few bucks here and there.

Sit down and map out how much free time you have each week. You could make a chart like this:

FREE TIME SCHEDULE

Time	Monday - Friday	Saturday	Sunday
8 am			
Noon			
4 pm			
8 pm			

Money Makers

As of summer 2008, the national **minimum wage** was $6.55 per hour. The state with one of the highest minimum wages is the state of Washington. There, in 2008, it was $8.07. If you have a job where you earn tips for giving good service, you can make even more each hour.

Think how many of these hours are already filled with getting ready for school, being in class, doing homework, participating in sports, helping out at home, and hanging out with your friends. For many jobs, you would need at least two free hours in a row on any given day to be able to work somewhere. Do you have enough time left over to work?

Like everything else in life, taking a job has advantages and disadvantages. Let's take a look at some of them.

The Positives

What are the benefits of having a job? Did you say, MONEY?

Money is one of the biggest reasons to work, but it is not the only one. Here are a few others that are just as important—or even more so:

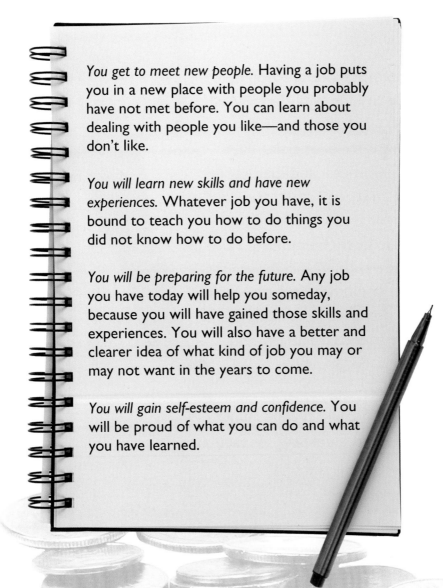

You get to meet new people. Having a job puts you in a new place with people you probably have not met before. You can learn about dealing with people you like—and those you don't like.

You will learn new skills and have new experiences. Whatever job you have, it is bound to teach you how to do things you did not know how to do before.

You will be preparing for the future. Any job you have today will help you someday, because you will have gained those skills and experiences. You will also have a better and clearer idea of what kind of job you may or may not want in the years to come.

You will gain self-esteem and confidence. You will be proud of what you can do and what you have learned.

If making money is one of your biggest reasons for taking a job, then be sure to figure out just how much you will earn. That way, you can decide if your time and efforts will be well spent. Here is how you can figure out your weekly pay:

# of hours worked per week x amount being paid per hour = weekly pay

Since most jobs are not available to kids until they are at least 14, what can you do now if you want to learn skills, have new experiences, and make some money? First, you could ask your parents for extra chores around the house in exchange for a raise in your allowance. Think about jobs that you could do that you aren't already doing for your family, or for your friends, relatives, and neighbors. For example:

- washing and folding laundry
- dusting, sweeping, or vacuuming
- taking out the trash
- babysitting
- dogsitting
- washing dishes
- walking the dog

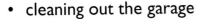
- cleaning out the garage
- cleaning out the closets
- mowing the lawn
- shoveling snow
- raking leaves
- washing and waxing the car
- washing windows
- running errands
- taking care of a garden (watering, weeding, etc.)
- delivering newspapers
- tutoring other students
- providing computer services
- typing papers
- taking photographs
- teaching others how to do something you are exceptionally good at doing

Talk to people about what they need help with the most. Ask others you know how you might help them. Talk to your neighbors. Call your grandparents or other relatives if they live nearby. Are there any elderly people in your area? Any families with a new baby? Often they need help doing things that would be easy for you to do. You would help someone and get some money from it—a win-win situation all around.

Washing your dog or someone else's dog can be a great way to earn money—although a wet one. Be sure that you wear the right clothes for the job you choose to do!

The Negatives

There are some downsides to working, too. They deserve your thought as well.

Working can cut into your fun time. Whatever type of job you get and however many hours you work per week, you will have to give up that time from somewhere else. You might not get to spend as much time being with your friends, reading

Taking a job will leave you with less time for doing other things. Spending time with your family is always important, so make sure you can fit it in even if your schedule changes.

books, watching television, or playing games. Those hours will now be spent working.

Working can cut into your study time. You may not have as much time to do your homework and to study as you did before, and your grades could slip. It is important you do not let this happen.

Working can cut into your sleep time. You may find yourself giving up an hour or two of sleep each night in order to fit everything in. This is dangerous. Not enough sleep takes from your ability to concentrate, and it puts your health at risk.

Don't let this be you! Make sure you have enough time for sleep, studying, and being with friends and family.

Getting any kind of job—from the ones you take now to the ones that have to wait until you are a teenager, will involve your parents. You will need their permission— and often their help—to get a job. Sit down and explain your reasons for wanting to

Your parents are one of the best resources for making job plans. Sit down and talk to them, and they may just surprise you with the ideas they have for you!

One of the best parts of trying out different jobs now is that it will help you figure out what you want to do in the future. Perhaps you will be a pilot or a doctor!

work. Show them the thought you have given to this idea. They may be quite impressed with your **maturity** and **dedication**. They may also have some ideas, suggestions, and tips that you had not yet thought about.

If a job is in your near future, let's take a look at how you can find a job that best suits you.

21

THE WORK FOR WORK BEGINS

Before you can go to work, you have to do some work! Sit down and think long and hard about what kind of job would be best for you. After all, everyone is different. People have different personalities, likes, and dislikes. They will not all fit the same way in different kinds of jobs.

Asking Some Questions

How do you know what kind of work would suit you the best? Start by asking yourself some serious questions.

- What is my favorite class in school?
- What do I like to do the most in my free time? What are my hobbies?
- What talents do I already have? What knowledge do I already have?
- Do I like working alone or with a team?
- Do I prefer to be inside or outside the most?
- What are my biggest strengths and weaknesses?

- What kinds of jobs look exciting and which ones do not?
- What kind of career do I want when I am an adult?

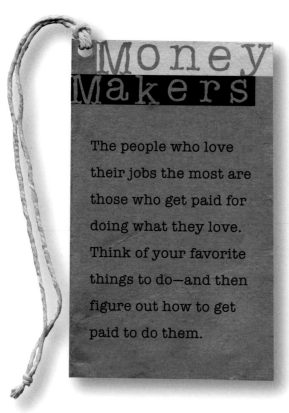

Money Makers

The people who love their jobs the most are those who get paid for doing what they love. Think of your favorite things to do—and then figure out how to get paid to do them.

Think about your answers and what they reveal about you. Talk to your parents about them and see if they agree. Talk to your friends and get their opinions about you. You might even want to ask some of your teachers.

Being Your Own Boss

One way to make sure you get hired for a job that you enjoy is to be your own boss. A person who starts his or her own business is called an **entrepreneur**.

Creating your own business can be exciting—and scary too. It takes dedication, courage, independence, and leadership. It also takes time and responsibility. What happens if your weekend juice stand is so successful that it turns into something you provide every afternoon? What if word of your great baby-sitting abilities spreads and suddenly you are booked every weekend for the next two months, plus Wednesday and Friday afternoons? Perhaps the people you mow the lawn for share your name with their friends, and suddenly people are calling all summer long asking you if you're available for additional work! It sounds wonderful—and it certainly can be, but it also means you have less free time to do the things you want to do. Remember that free time chart you made? (See page 14.) It might need to be updated as your business booms.

Before you start dreaming of being the best dog walker in the state, be sure to think about the following:

Money Makers

When Krysta Morlan was in tenth grade, she invented a device that helps cool off people who are wearing casts. It pumps air through a plastic tube and makes wearing a cast much more comfortable. Read more about Krysta at http://web.mit.edu/invent/a-winners/a-morlan.html.

- How old do you have to be to do this job?
- Is this work seasonal, or could you do it year round?
- What skills and/or training do you need?
- How much money do you need to get started or to buy supplies?
- What equipment do you need? Do you have it already or will you have to buy it?
- Do you need a partner or can you do this alone?
- Do you need parental permission? (Hint: The answer here is always yes!)

- What time of day can you do this job? Does this fit with your schedule?
- Is this job safe? Are there any dangers you need to be aware of?
- Will you be able to stick with this job and follow through for your customers?

After you see how well you like the job, you might decide to make it a business. If you do, the next step is creating a business plan. Just as you would not take a trip somewhere new without a map, you should not start a business without a plan.

Planning It Out

A business plan takes a lot of time and effort, but it will help keep your business on track—and profitable. Here are the steps you need to do to make your plan:

Choose a name for your business. Make it a catchy one that people will remember. For example, if you are going to start a car-washing business, you could name it Car Washes for Less. Not many people would remember that, however. But what if you named it Wash and Dash or Krazy Kids' Car Wash? These would catch people's attention.

Figure out your goal or mission. If you are starting a car wash, for example, clearly your goal is to get the dirt off cars, but it should go beyond that. You want to make sure they are thoroughly clean—and that your customers are happy. Will you dry the cars off? Wash the windows? Vacuum the inside? This should all be part of your plan.

Figure your basic budget. Make a list of all the equipment and supplies you will need. Don't forget to list the cost of advertising or paying a friend to help. Check off the ones you already have and make a separate list of those you need to buy. Find out how much they cost, and use that number to help figure out your budget. For example, for a car wash, you will need a hose, water, soap, wax, towels, window cleaner, paper towels, buckets, and rags. Most likely, your family already has a hose and a small hand vacuum. Water and electricity come from the house—with your parents' permission. You go to the local hardware store and buy the rest, which costs $52.00. These supplies are enough to wash 10 cars.

Money spent: $52.00

Car wash price: $5.00

10 washes x $5.00 = $50.00

Uh-oh. Not only did you make $2 less than you spent on supplies, but what about the cost to your parents for water and electricity? What about you? You should be paid for your time. Clearly, you will need to either charge more for your services (and is a car wash going to be worth more than $5 to people?) or reduce the cost of your supplies (buy in bulk, go to discount stores, recycle, etc.). Otherwise, you are working and losing money with every moment. If you are not sure what to charge, look around and see what other places are charging. Talk to your parents and friends about how to cut costs.

Washing cars is another wet job, so make sure you have the right clothes on! Summertime is the best time for a job like this because the hot sun keeps you warm and helps the cars dry much faster.

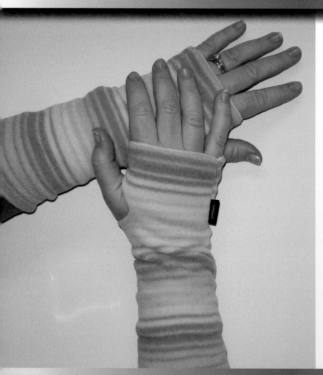

Not sure a kid can be an entrepreneur? Ask K K Gregory. When she was ten years old, she invented Wristies®, fingerless gloves that are worn under mittens to keep wrists warm and prevent snow from getting into coat sleeves. Today, she has her own business and is going strong! Check it out at www.wristies.com.

Keep track of your profit and loss. A record will show you if you are making a profit or if you're losing money—and how much. A simple notebook is all you need. You could create a page that looks something like this:

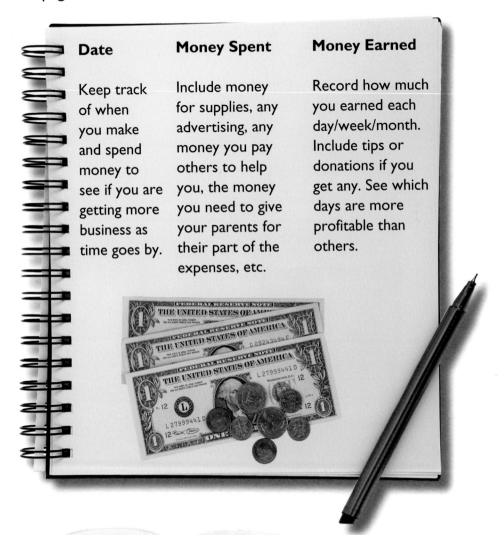

Date	Money Spent	Money Earned
Keep track of when you make and spend money to see if you are getting more business as time goes by.	Include money for supplies, any advertising, any money you pay others to help you, the money you need to give your parents for their part of the expenses, etc.	Record how much you earned each day/week/month. Include tips or donations if you get any. See which days are more profitable than others.

As you can see, getting or creating jobs requires doing your homework first. It takes time and effort to make money—but that is what earning is all about!

Having your own money that you worked hard to earn can give you a wonderful feeling. It is what keeps people of all ages going to work every day.

Chapter 4

WHY WAIT? LEGAL MATTERS

Although the best options for you to earn money right now might be starting a pet-sitting service or a car wash or selling your invention or doing any of the many projects discussed earlier in this book, as you get older, you may want to work for someone else. Why do you have to wait a few years before you can go out and get a "real" job? It's the law. Waiting may be hard, but by following the steps outlined in this book, you will already be way ahead of many other kids who never experience any kind of job until they turn sixteen and get hired.

There are a number of laws that tell you what you are and are not allowed to do when you start working. These laws are determined by the national **Fair Labor Standards Act** (FLSA). They clearly list what **minors** (people under the age of 18)

can and cannot do, what hours they can work, and what time of day they can work. When you apply for a job, you will have to prove your age. You can do this with one of the following:

- birth certificate
- driver's license
- notarized statement from parents/legal guardians
- baptismal record

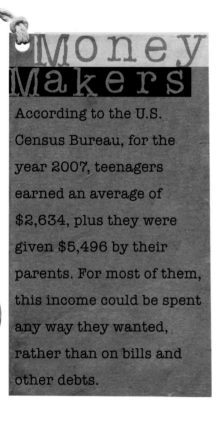

Money Makers

According to the U.S. Census Bureau, for the year 2007, teenagers earned an average of $2,634, plus they were given $5,496 by their parents. For most of them, this income could be spent any way they wanted, rather than on bills and other debts.

If you are under the age of 18, you will also have to have a work permit before you can start your new job. To get one of these, you and one of your parents must meet with a permit officer. You can usually find one at your school or look them up in the Yellow Pages of the telephone book. Be sure to have your birth certificate, social security card, and a statement from the employer that lists the job's duties, hours of work, and your parent's consent. When everything is in order, and after paying a small fee (usually $5 or less), you will be given the permit, plus two copies: one for your employer and one for your school.

Now, let's take a look at these FLSA laws:

- 10- and 11-year-olds may perform jobs on farms owned or operated by their parents outside of school hours in **nonhazardous** jobs
- 12- and 13-year-olds may work outside of school hours in nonhazardous jobs with a parent's written consent
- 14- and 15-year-olds may perform any nonhazardous farm job outside of school hours
- 16-year-olds and older may perform any job, whether hazardous or not, for unlimited hours

If you are under 14, you can also do the following:

- Deliver newspapers
- Perform on the radio, television, movies or theatrical productions
- Work for your parents in their non-farm business

Hours of Employment

Fourteen- and 15-year-olds may be employed outside of school hours for a limited amount of time.

work	school in session	school out of session
hours per day	3	8
hours per week	18	40

They may not work before 7:00 A.M. or after 7:00 P.M., except in summertime (June 1 through Labor Day). Then they can work until 9:00 P.M. They may not work more than 4 hours without a 30-minute uninterrupted meal period—you have to have time

to eat! You also are required, by law, to take a paid rest break of at least 10 minutes for every 2 hours worked.

Sixteen- and 17-year-olds may be employed for unlimited hours. There are no federal laws restricting the number of hours of work per day or per week. They are entitled by law to uninterrupted meal times of at least 30 minutes when working more than five hours a day. They are also allowed at least a 10-minute paid rest break for each four hours worked.

There are more than a dozen prohibited jobs for people under the age of 18:

- manufacturing or storing explosives
- driving a motor vehicle or being an outside helper on a motor vehicle
- logging and sawmilling
- operating power-driven woodworking machines
- risking exposure to **radioactive** substances and to **ionizing** radiations
- operating power-driven hoisting equipment
- mining
- meat packing or processing
- operating power-driven bakery machines
- operating power-driven paper products machines
- manufacturing brick, tile, and related products
- operating power-driven circular saws, band saws, and guillotine shears
- performing wrecking, demolition, and ship-breaking operations
- roofing operations
- excavation/digging operations

Guillotine shears have a long sharp blade that drops down quickly to cut tough or thick material such as sheet metal. No one under 18 is allowed to operate this type of machine. According to the National Institute for Occupational Safety and Health, every year, 60 to 70 teenagers are killed in a workplace injury. Getting a job is great—but staying safe at work is even more important. Know the safety rules of any job you take and follow them closely!

These are the federal child labor laws. They apply to all young people, even those students who are homeschooled.

There are also state-based labor laws. Check your state labor laws at the U.S. Department of Labor web site:

http://www.dol.gov/esa/programs/whd/state/state.htm

Breaking any of these laws is not good for you or for your employer. If caught, you will lose your job, and your employer may have to pay hundreds or thousands of dollars in fines.

Paying the Government

There is one more kind of law you should know about when you enter the working world: paying income taxes. There are several types of income tax: federal income tax, state income tax, **Social Security** tax, and **Medicare** tax. Sometimes there are local taxes, too. Federal and state taxes help pay for things like national defense, police service, schools, highway repair, and other state and national programs. In 2007, you could earn up to $5,350 before you would owe federal income tax. Each state had its own minimum-income tax laws. Anyone who earned over $400 had to pay Social Security and Medicare taxes.

Social Security, Medicare, and federal income taxes are sent to the **Internal Revenue Service** (IRS), and state taxes are sent to the state treasurer. If you work for a company, part of each paycheck will be held back for taxes and sent in for you. If you work for yourself, however, it is up to you to send money in to the IRS and the state treasurer. If your business happens to make a *lot* of profit, you have to pay **quarterly taxes** or you will be charged penalties.

In April, when you file your taxes, you will find out whether you paid too much or too little in taxes for the previous year. If you overpaid, the extra money will be returned to you in a **tax refund**. If you paid too little, you might owe penalties and interest as well as the tax.

Where to Find a Job

If you're ready to start working for someone else, there are many places to look for job openings.

Read the ads in your local newspaper.

Check with your city's employment agencies.

Look online at ads.

Look on bulletin boards for ads. For example:

Public libraries
School libraries
Grocery stores
Coffee houses
Bookstores
Schools
Day care centers
Teacher supply stores

⚠ WARNING

Never, ever agree to meet a stranger alone. Have your parents go with you until they are comfortable with the person who has hired you.

When you weigh what you have to do to find a job and keep it against what you have earned, was it worth it? Be sure to consider what you have gained through this experience besides money.

Money Makers

For any job interview, be sure to dress neatly and professionally. Make sure your hair is brushed, you're nice and clean, and you mind your manners.

Getting Paid

When your first paycheck comes, it can be pretty exciting.

Remember that you may be paid in cash, personal check, business check, money order, or even a direct deposit into your bank account. Some places pay weekly, while others may pay you every two or even four weeks. Be sure that you know these details ahead of time so you are not surprised or confused. Also, take a moment to think about how much you made in one week's time. Think about how much time it took to earn it. Weigh in what you will do with the money and what sacrifices you had to make to earn it. Now, ask yourself: Is the amount of money I made worth the time and effort it took? That is a decision only you can make.

Was the class able to raise the money they needed?

WE DID IT!

Chapter 5

SCIENCE MUSEUM, HERE WE COME!

The school bus was as full of noise as it was of students. The day to go to the science museum had finally arrived! For weeks, the kids had worked hard to get Astrid to the top of that mountain. Mr. Franks was proud of each and every one of them. Not only had they raised enough to pay for all of their tickets, but they had enough left over to make sure everyone could stop in the lab's deli for a slice of pizza and a drink.

"It was fun washing all those cars," Carlos said to Philip. "I think we must have the

Money Makers

Remember that when you babysit, you have a big responsibility to take good care of young children. Always have a list of emergency contacts by the phone. Know where the parents can be reached and when they are supposed to come back home.

cleanest block in the entire neighborhood."

"My babysitting job rocked," said Melanie. "I have jobs lined up for the next three weeks."

"What about you, Carter? How was the leaf-raking business?" asked Mr. Franks.

Carter chuckled and held up his hands. "I think I got a blister for every dollar I earned," he said. "But I helped a lot of people, and I am glad!"

"I found it really hard to fit in extra work between school and sports," admitted Tomás. "I think I understand why my parents are so tired by the end of the day."

Mr. Franks saw Lucas grinning. "What's so funny, Lucas?" he asked.

"Well, Mr. Franks," said Lucas, "I want you to know I tried my very best, but no matter how many signs I put up, I never was able to sell my sister!"

The entire class laughed, including Mr. Franks. It was clear that a lot of important lessons had been learned long before they walked into the museum.

FOR SALE

Baby Sister: Comes complete with bottles, diapers and toys.

Selling a brother or sister may sound like a good plan—but you can bet that your parents won't give you permission for this idea.

Books

Albrektson, J. Raymond, *Money-Savvy Kids: Parenting Penny Wise Kids in a Money Hungry World.* Colorado Springs: Waterbrook Press, 2002.

Brown, Jeff. *The Kids' Guide to Business.* Seattle, Washington: Teaching Kids Business.com, 2003.

Burkett, Larry. *Money Matters for Kids.* Chicago: Moody Publishers, 2001.

Drobot, Eve. *Money, Money, Money: Where It Comes From, How to Save It, Spend It and Make It.* Toronto, Ontario: Maple Tree Press, 2004.

Harman, Hollis Page. *Money Sense for Kids.*: Hauppauge, New York: Barron's Educational Series, 2005.

Linecker, Adelia C., and Sandra Lamb. *What Color Is Your Piggy Bank? Entrepreneurial Ideas for Self -Starting Kids.* Montreal, Québec, Canada: Lobster Press, 2004.

Mayr, Diane. *The Everything Kids' Money Book: From Saving to Spending to Investing.* Cincinnati: Adams Media Corp., 2002.

Works Consulted

Bochner, Arthur, and Rose Bochner. *The New Totally Awesome Money Book for Kids.* New York: New Market Press, 2007.

Child Labor Coalition: Child Labor in the U.S.
http://www.stopchildlabor.org/USchildlabor/fact1.htm

Labor Law Center: State and Federal Minimum Wage Rates
http://www.laborlawcenter.com/state-Minimum-Wage-rates.
asp?gclid=CI6V9LLjt5ECFRdPagodVH0hCg

Lermitte, Paul. *Making Allowances: A Dollars and Sense Guide to Teaching Kids about Money.* Columbus, Ohio: McGraw-Hill, 2002.

MoneyInstructor.com: Ways for Kids to Make Money
http://www.moneyinstructor.com/art/waysforkids.asp

The Motley Fool: "How Kids Can Earn Money," January 9, 2006,
http://www.fool.com/personal-finance/retirement/2006/01/09/
how-kids-can-earn-money.aspx

Oliveri, Denise. "Summer Jobs for Kids: Ways for Tweens to Make Money," May 11, 2007.
http://parentingtweens.suite101.com/article.cfm/
summer_jobs_for_kids

Shelley, Susan. *Complete Idiot's Guide to Money for Teens.* Fort Smith, Arizona: Alpha Books, 2001.

Ways for Kids to Earn Money; Family Education.com
http://life.familyeducation.com/money-and-kids/
money-management/47555.html

Women's Finance: Helping Kids Earn Extra Money
http://www.womens-finance.com/kidsfinances/
earnextra.shtml

On the Internet

PBS Kids. Games: "Be Your Own Boss"
http://pbskids.org/itsmylife/games/boss/

Planet Orange: Where Kids Learn About Earning, Spending,
Saving, and Investing
http://www.orangekids.com/

The Motley Fool: Kids Earning Money
http://www.fool.com/foolu/askfoolu/2002/
askfoolu021218.htm

The Mint
http://www.themint.org/kids/index.html

Kids.gov: Earning Money
http://www.kids.gov/6_8/6_8_money_earning.shtml

Glossary

dedication (deh-dih-KAY-shun)—Willingness to stick to something, even if it is hard to do so.

entrepreneur (on-treh-preh-NOOR)—A person who creates and runs his or her own business.

Fair Labor Standards Act—An act passed in 1938 that sets up a national minimum wage, requires recordkeeping for employers, and outlines legal working hours and laws for employing minors.

Internal Revenue (REH-veh-noo) **Service**—The branch of the U.S. Department of the Treasury that collects income taxes each year.

ionizing (EYE-uh-ny-zing)—Able to give an electrical charge in one's body.

maturity (muh-CHUR-ih-tee)—Being fully responsible in thoughts and actions.

Medicare (MEH-dih-kayr)—The federal program that provides health insurance to senior citizens, the disabled, and some disadvantaged children, among others.

minimum wage—The least amount of money an employer must pay a worker per hour. Some states do not participate.

minor (MY-nur)—A person under the age of 18 years old.

nonhazardous (non-HAA-zur-dus)—Not dangerous.

quarterly taxes (KWAR-ter-ly TAK-ses)—Money that is paid to the IRS for income earned per quarter year (every three months).

radioactive (ray-dee-oh-AK-tiv)—Emitting harmful particles of energy.

Social Security (SOH-shul seh-KYUR-ih-tee)—A government-based program that sends people money to live on after they retire.

tax refund (REE-fund)—The money the IRS sends back to someone if he or she paid more taxes than was required during the year.

Index